GIZMO
Goes to Yellowstone

Copyright © 2024 Heidi Heisel

All rights reserved. No part of this publication may be reproduced, distributed or transmitted in any form or by any means, including photocopying, recording, or other electronic or mechanical methods, without the prior written permission of the author.

eBook Designed by

Dedication

The book is dedicated to all of our furry friends who teach us everyday how to love unconditionally

I found Gizmo on I-10. A little ball of white fur about to merge with traffic. One slam of the brakes and both of our lives changed forever.

Gizmo doesn't have a tail,
and he doesn't know why.
He can't remember having one,
but wants to give it a try.

Sometimes it's fun to be different,
but sometimes you want to fit in.
Gizmo wanted his very own tail,
to wag with all of his friends.

But where do you go,
when you decide you want one too?
There isn't an online store,
and they don't sell them at the zoo.

Someone once told him,
where deer and antelope roam,
where bears, wolves, and buffalo,
all call Yellowstone home.

Surely someone there must know,
where one might find a tail.
The answers had to be there,
on that Yellowstone Trail.

Yellowstone was magical,
beautiful and vast.
Waterfalls and wildlife,
lots of herds to ask.

First came the antelope,
whose tails were barely there.
They were hidden on their backsides,
where it's kind of rude to stare.

Then came a herd of deer,
whose tails were short and white.
They stood up when they ran,
but the wag, it wasn't right.

Gizmo got discouraged,
but no giving up just yet.
He had to keep on looking.
To quit, might mean regret.

Gizmo saw some buffalo,
who had heard about his plight.
They spread the word around the park,
to find the tail just right.

The buffalo tails were long and skinny,
great for swatting flies.
But way too long for Gizmo,
they weren't the right size.

Then down from the sky,
a raven stopped to chat.
He flapped his wings and bragged,
that feathers are where it's at.

"With feathers for a tail,
you may not get a wag,
Buy maybe you could learn to fly,
then you, yourself can brag."

Gizmo thanked the raven,
and then politely declined.
He wanted a tail to fit in,
and feathers, they weren't the right kind.

Gizmo talked to a wolf,
whose tail had perfect wag.
It was big, bushy, and long,
but on Gizmo it would drag.

Gizmo's legs were way to short
for any tail that long.
He had to find one smaller,
one that looks like it belongs.

Finally near Old Faithful,
Gizmo caught a break.
He found a white bunny tail,
and he thought it looked great!

It didn't have a wag,
but it did have a poof.
He could wiggle it a little,
but he looked a little like a goof.

Gizmo said his goodbyes,
and showed off his new wiggle.
It was cute, but funny too.
They tried hard not to giggle.

Gizmo felt embarrassed.
He thought he'd found the one.
Now he was even more different,
and they were making fun.

Gizmo took off the poof.
He had to search some more.
Out there was his perfect tail,
the one he was longing for.

Then through the trees,
A huge grizzly bear appeared.
He was massive and moving fast.
Gizmo was really scared.

The Grizzly looked at Gizmo,
then stared at his rear end.
"I hear you're looking for a tail
to be like all of your friends.

I came to give you my advice;
That is to just do you.
No one else can do it
better than you can do.

Some want to fit in,
and that's just fine,
but the ones who stand out,
those are my kind.

They don't go with the flow,
like old dead fish do.
They do their best.
They think things through.

Be who you are.
Learn when you fail.
Life will reward you,
with more than a tail."

As that Grizzly walked away,
Gizmo slowly exhaled.
But he smiled when he saw it,
He didn't have a Tail.

Illustrated By River Wilson

River Wilson illustrated Gizmo Goes to Yellowstone at the age of 12. As an aspiring artist, River accepted the challenge of illustrating Gizmo's adventures, as told by Gimzo. River is currently attending the University of North Texas with a Major in Marketing. He has a passion for design and creating new things. He loves to travel and has explored 13 countries so far.

Written By Heidi Phillips

Heidi Heisel has been Gizmo's mom ever since she found him on the freeway many years ago. Being a photographer, Heidi has traveled to many beautiful places with Gizmo by her side.. They have shared many adventures and taken lots of pictures of National Parks, and even Europe. Now we are sharing the stories, from Gizmo's point of view.

www.ingramcontent.com/pod-product-compliance
Lightning Source LLC
Chambersburg PA
CBHW041505220426
43661CB00016B/1258